Pony-Mad Princess

Princess Ellie
and the Palace Plot

Kate looked thoughtful. "Maybe Lord Leo doesn't really know anything about horses. That would explain why he hooted at Angel yesterday and frightened her."

"But that would mean he's making it all up," said Ellie. "And if he's lying about the horses, maybe he's lying about other things as well…"

Look out for more sparkly adventures of

The Pony-Mad Princess!

The Pony-Mad Princess

Schools' Service

Princess Ellie
and the Palace Plot

Diana Kimpton
Illustrated by Lizzie Finlay

USBORNE

For Graham

First published in 2005 by Usborne Publishing Ltd., Usborne House,
83-85 Saffron Hill, London EC1N 8RT, England. www.usborne.com

Based on an original concept by Anne Finnis.

A CIP catalogue record for this book is available from the British Library.

JFMAMJJAS ND/06

N 0 7460 6733 X

d in Great Britain.

Chapter 1

"Come on, Angel," said Princess Ellie,
patting the skewbald foal's brown and white
neck. Angel's tiny hooves crunched on the
gravel as she walked up the palace drive.
Ellie was on one side of the foal and her
best friend, Kate, was on the other.

Kate grinned. "She's getting good at
being led." She held up the lead rope to

show how slack it was. "Look! She's not pulling at all."

"We could try going faster," suggested Ellie. "But that's up to you. She's your pony."

Kate made a clicking noise with her tongue and started to run. Angel pricked up her ears, arched her neck and broke into a trot.

Suddenly, Ellie heard the sound of an engine. She looked round quickly and saw a bright red sports car racing up behind them. She waved at it to slow down. To her annoyance, the driver just waved back. He didn't adjust his speed at all. Ellie waved again, more urgently this time. Surely he could see Angel was only a foal. She wasn't used to traffic.

But the driver still took no notice. He gave a long, loud blast on the car's horn. Then he roared past, waving cheerfully. The wheels of the red car sent up a shower of gravel.

The combination of the noise, the speed and the stinging stones was too much for Angel. She jumped away from the bright red monster and nearly knocked Kate over. Then she threw herself backwards, pulling hard on the rope and trying to break free.

Ellie lunged forward and grabbed hold of Angel's headcollar. "Steady, girl," she said in a soothing voice. "It's gone now."

"There's nothing to be frightened of," added Kate, gently stroking the foal's face.

The Pony-Mad Princess

Angel relaxed a little. She stopped trying to pull away, but she was obviously still scared. She was breathing fast, and her neck was damp with sweat.

There was no sign of the car now. It had sped away towards the palace and disappeared round a bend. Ellie glowered after it. "Silly fool! I wonder who he is."

Kate looked thoughtful. "The guards at

the gate let him in so he must be visiting someone at the palace."

"That's true," replied Ellie. "But he obviously doesn't know anything about horses or he wouldn't have frightened Angel."

Kate turned the foal towards the stables. "Let's get out of the way quickly before he comes back."

Meg, the palace groom, was sweeping the yard when they arrived. She stopped as soon as she saw them and asked, "How did Angel's lesson go?" Then she listened with concern as Ellie and Kate described what had happened. "Thank goodness she wasn't hurt," she said, when they had finished.

"She could have been if she'd run away," said Kate. "She was really scared."

"But she's calmed down now," said Ellie. "Shall we turn her out in the field with Starlight?"

"That's a good idea," said Meg. "She'll be pleased to be back with her mum."

Starlight whinnied a welcome and trotted to the gate to meet her daughter. As soon as Kate had unfastened Angel's headcollar, the two of them cantered side by side to their favourite spot in the shade of the oak tree.

Princess Ellie and the Palace Plot

Starlight was the largest of Ellie's five ponies but Angel's spindly legs were so long that she could easily keep up with her mother.

The other four ponies were standing on the far side of the field, swishing their tails gently to keep the flies away. Shadow, the greedy Shetland, was the only one eating the grass. His best friend, Sundance, dozed beside him while Moonbeam and Rainbow stood side by side, watching Angel.

Suddenly a polite cough made Ellie jump and a deep voice said, "Excuse me, Princess Aurelia."

She spun round and saw Higginbottom, the butler, standing behind her. She'd been so busy watching the ponies that she hadn't heard his footsteps on the grass.

The Pony-Mad Princess

Higginbottom gave a deep bow. As usual he was wearing his black evening suit and white gloves. She had never seen him in any other clothes and she had never managed to persuade him to call her Ellie. Like everyone else at the palace, he insisted on calling her by her real name.

He straightened up and announced, "The King and Queen would like you to join them for tea in the parlour as soon as possible. The new royal designer has arrived and they want you to meet him."

"Bother," said Ellie. "Why now?" she thought. She hated having to miss time at the stables. "I was going to clean Starlight's saddle before supper."

"Never mind," said Kate. "It can wait until tomorrow. And the royal designer might be interesting. I wonder what he's going to design?"

"No one's told me yet," replied Ellie. She suddenly felt very keen to find out. But as she ran back to the palace, she remembered the horrid driver of the red sports car. "I hope he's not the designer," she thought. She'd already seen enough of that man for one day.

Chapter 2

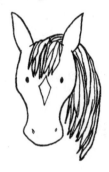

Ellie ran indoors and nearly bumped into her governess, Miss Stringle.

"Where are you going in such a rush?" she asked.

"To the parlour," explained Ellie. "Mum and Dad said I've got to go there straight away. The new designer's arrived."

Miss Stringle was unimpressed. "That is

no reason to run. There is always time for a princess to walk in a dignified manner." She paused and wrinkled her nose in disgust.

"And there's always time to change out of your riding clothes."

Ellie sighed. No one else in the palace seemed to like the smell of horse as much as she did. She walked sedately up the spiral staircase to her room until she was out of Miss Stringle's sight. Then she ran up the remaining steps, two at a time.

15

The Pony-Mad Princess

Inside her very pink bedroom, she pulled off her stable clothes and wiped the dirt off her face with a wet flannel. Then she put on a frilly, pink dress, swapped her everyday crown for a tiara and hurried down to the parlour.

Despite her rush, she couldn't resist stopping at a small table beside the double doors. Standing in the middle of it was her favourite ornament – a beautiful statue of a flying horse made from pure gold. Its glittering wings were encrusted with diamonds and its eyes were clear, blue sapphires.

She gazed at it for a moment. Then she forced herself to turn away. Her parents were waiting for her and she didn't want to get into trouble by being late. She smoothed the front of her skirt, swung open the doors and stepped into the parlour.

The King and Queen smiled at her as she walked in. They were standing beside the marble fireplace, talking to a man who looked horribly familiar. Ellie recognized him immediately. He was the driver of the car.

"Let me introduce you to my daughter," said the King.

"How divine," said the visitor. He stepped swiftly to Ellie's side, took her hand in his and gave a very theatrical bow. "Lord Leo of Vincent at your service, Your Highness."

"Hello," replied Ellie. She didn't say she was pleased to meet him because she

wasn't. She'd taken an instant dislike to the man as soon as he'd frightened Angel.

The Queen obviously felt much more enthusiastic about the new designer. "We're so lucky Lord Leo saw our advertisement," she declared in an excited voice. "He's related to Leonardo da Vinci."

"Who's he?" asked Ellie. She was sure she'd heard the name before, but she couldn't remember where.

"Oh dear," said the King. "I must ask Miss Stringle to spend more time on your art lessons. Leonardo da Vinci is one of the most famous artists in the whole world."

"And he's my great-great-great-great-great-grandfather," boasted Lord Leo. "I'm so lucky to have inherited his talent." He started to walk in a circle around Ellie, staring at her intently as if she was an object in a museum. "How absolutely charming. I just love those curls and that dress is so very, very…" He hesitated for a moment, as if he was searching for the right word.

"Pink?" suggested Ellie.

"That's it," he cried, waving his hands dramatically in the air to emphasize his words. "It's so very pink. So absolutely, completely and utterly pink."

19

The Pony-Mad Princess

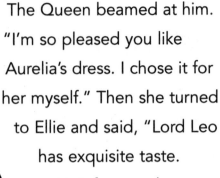

The Queen beamed at him. "I'm so pleased you like Aurelia's dress. I chose it for her myself." Then she turned to Ellie and said, "Lord Leo has exquisite taste. He's from such an important artistic family."

"He's the perfect person to be our royal designer," explained the King. "He agrees with me completely that we need to bring the royal family up to date. So he's going to give us a makeover just like they do on TV."

"Oh," said Ellie, trying to sound more enthusiastic than she felt. So that's what the designer was going to do. She wished her parents had never started watching those lifestyle programmes. Before they had, they'd been quite content with everything the way it was. Now they were convinced that the royal family needed to change its image.

Ellie wasn't sure she wanted *her* image changed by someone who dressed in such a peculiar way. Lord Leo was wearing a green velvet suit, green shoes, green socks and a green silk shirt with ruffles round the neck. If he'd been smaller, he would have looked like a leprechaun. But he wasn't. He was so tall and thin that he looked more like a giant green bean.

The conversation was interrupted by the arrival of Higginbottom carrying a large tray. It was laden with cups and saucers, a silver teapot and a plate of dainty iced cakes. Kate's grandmother had obviously been busy in the kitchen. She was the palace cook.

Lord Leo screwed up his face in disgust. "Oh dear," he said, as he pointed to Higginbottom's evening suit. "Black is so last year."

"But butlers always wear black," said the King. "It's a tradition."

"Nonsense," declared Lord Leo. "Traditions are for breaking. If you want to bring the royal family up to date, you've got to let go of the past."

"Are you sure?" asked the Queen.

"Absolutely," said Lord Leo. "You can't have a makeover without change."

To Ellie's surprise, the King and Queen nodded agreement without any more

22

argument. Lord Leo seemed to know exactly the right way to persuade them and they were so impressed by his ancestry that they believed everything he said.

That gave Ellie an idea. "Is pink last year too?" she asked. Perhaps he could persuade her parents to redecorate her very pink bedroom.

"Absolutely not," gushed the designer. "Pink is perfection, especially for princesses."

Ellie's shoulders sagged with disappointment. She'd liked the colour when she was small but she didn't like it any more. She was trying to persuade her parents that she preferred purple. Lord Leo's opinion would make that task much harder.

She took a cake to cheer herself up and

gazed through the window while she nibbled the icing. The red sports car was parked outside. Its number plate said LEO 1.

Ellie scowled at it. Her parents obviously thought Lord Leo was charming, but she didn't. He was a bad driver, he had bad taste, and he knew nothing at all about ponies. What sort of mess was he going to make of her home?

Chapter 3

The next morning, Ellie was relieved to find that everything in the palace looked the same as usual. Lord Leo hadn't had time to make any changes yet.

She was less pleased when Miss Stringle told her to write a story without any ponies in it. How could she possibly make that interesting? She chewed the end of her pencil thoughtfully and stared out of the window in search of ideas.

She couldn't see the stables from here but she did see a bright yellow delivery van arrive at the palace. The blue writing on its side announced that it contained "Fantastic Fashions for the Fabulous".

"I wonder what's in there," muttered Ellie.

"It's probably something to do with that dreadful man," replied Miss Stringle as she peered out of the window.

Ellie stared at her in surprise. "Don't you like Lord Leo?" she asked.

"I certainly don't like his ideas," said Miss Stringle. "Royalty is not supposed to change. It's supposed to stay the same. So should palaces and so should governesses."

Ellie smiled. "Has he tried to change you?"

"Scarlet!" Miss Stringle spat the word out as if it tasted dreadful. "He wants *me* to wear *scarlet*. I told him that generations of palace governesses have always worn brown. But he insisted that brown was..."

"...so last year?" suggested Ellie.

"Exactly!" agreed Miss Stringle. "And I don't even care if he's right. Last year is fine for me and so is last century."

"I don't like him much either," said Ellie, quietly.

Her governess beamed. "It's so good to hear we agree about something, my dear." Then she hastily added, "But we must be polite to Lord Leo." She peered down at the blank piece of paper on Ellie's desk. "Maybe I've been a little harsh on you this morning. Although I don't want ponies in your story, I don't mind a few unicorns."

Ideas immediately flooded into Ellie's mind. Soon, she was so busy writing about a magical world that she was surprised when Miss Stringle told her to stop for lunch.

Ellie was even more surprised when she arrived at the dining room. The maid who opened the door wasn't in her usual uniform. Instead of a black dress, she was wearing a shimmery, purple one. Its long skirt was so tight and straight that she was finding it hard to walk. Ellie guessed the outfit was made by Fantastic Fashions for the Fabulous.

The maid tried to curtsey but the dress stopped her bending her knees properly and she nearly fell over. "Oops!" she groaned. "I'm afraid I haven't got the hang of this yet, Your Highness."

"Never mind, Susan," said Ellie. She felt sorry for her. She looked so uncomfortable.

Her parents were already sitting at the table, deep in conversation. The Queen looked up as Ellie sat down in her usual place. "Doesn't Susan's new uniform look fantastic?" she said.

"Are all the maids wearing purple now?" asked Ellie. She was pleased to see Lord Leo wasn't there. This was the first chance she'd had to speak to her parents on her own since he arrived.

"Oh, no," laughed the King. "Lord Leo has put all the maids in different colours. If they stand side by side, they look like a rainbow. It's wonderful."

"Are you sure?" asked Ellie. Then she added in a whisper, "Susan doesn't look very happy in her new outfit."

"Oh dear," said the Queen in a concerned voice. "I do hope she'll get used to it soon. Lord Leo promised us that everyone would."

Princess Ellie and the Palace Plot

"I'm not sure I will," said Ellie. "I wish
you'd stop Lord Leo changing everything."

"Nonsense!" said the King. "Change is
good. Change is exciting. We can't go on
living in the past for ever."

"And Lord Leo is the ideal designer for
us," added the Queen. "With such an
important ancestor, he's sure to organize
everything perfectly."

Ellie realized there was no point in arguing
with them. They had obviously made up their
minds and were completely captivated by
Lord Leo. So she walked across the room to
choose her lunch from the wonderful
selection of dishes laid out on the sideboard.
There were curls of ham stuffed with cream
cheese, chicken breasts roasted with truffles
and delicate meringue swans swimming on a

sea of thick chocolate sauce.

"What would you like to eat, Your Highness?" asked a man wearing a bright red jacket, white trousers and shiny, red boots that reached to his knees.

Ellie stared at him in astonishment. It was Higginbottom, the butler. "You do look different," she said. "I hardly recognized you."

Higginbottom looked embarrassed. "I hardly recognize myself," he muttered. "I look more like a lion tamer than a butler."

Ellie tried not to giggle. He was right. His outfit looked as if it had come straight from

32

a circus. But she couldn't imagine him telling an angry lion how to behave. He'd be more likely to offer it a sandwich. "Do you think you'll get used to it?" she asked, wondering if her mother was right.

"I suppose I will," answered Higginbottom. "But that doesn't mean I'll ever like it."

Ellie felt sorry for him and for all the maids. They didn't like Lord Leo's changes and neither did she. If only there was something she could do to stop him.

Chapter 4

Ellie had to go back to the schoolroom after lunch to finish her story. But as soon as Miss Stringle let her go, she rushed down to the stable yard. Meg had promised to give her a riding lesson that afternoon and she was keen to get started. She was also keen to tell Kate about Lord Leo but, to her disappointment, her friend wasn't waiting for her.

Princess Ellie and the Palace Plot

"Maybe the bus was late," suggested Meg. Kate lived at the palace with her grandparents because her parents worked abroad. But she went to school in the nearby village.

Meg picked up a box of grooming kit. "Let's get Sundance ready while we're waiting. I'm going to give you a lungeing lesson today."

Ellie felt confused. She knew lungeing was a good way to exercise a pony without getting on its back, but she couldn't see the point of doing it when she and Kate both wanted to ride. "I thought we were having a riding lesson," she complained.

"You are," laughed Meg. She held out a very long webbing strap. "I'll buckle one end of this lungeing-rein to Sundance and hold the other end in my hand. Then I'll make him go round me in a circle while you just concentrate on your riding."

Ellie was pleased that she would be riding after all, but she was worried that it might not be as easy as Meg made it sound. So she gave all her attention to grooming Sundance and tried not to think about what was coming next. Soon the chestnut pony's coat was gleaming and his feet shone with

hoof oil. Ellie fetched his saddle and bridle and put them on. "There's still no sign of Kate," she said, as she fastened his girth.

"We'd better start without her," said Meg. She picked up a headcollar with three large, brass rings attached to the noseband. "This is called the cavesson," she explained as she buckled it over the top of Sundance's bridle. Then she buckled the lungeing-rein to one of the rings and started to lead the chestnut pony out of the yard.

Ellie fetched her riding hat from the tack room and ran after Meg and Sundance. She caught them up just as they reached the sand school on the other side of the hay barn. It was a large rectangular area surrounded by a wooden fence. The thick layer of sand that covered the ground meant it was always soft enough to ride on, whatever the weather.

Meg waited while Ellie swung herself into the saddle. Then she tied the reins in a knot. "That will keep them out of the way," she explained. "You won't be needing those today." She told Sundance to walk on and used the lungeing-rein to guide him so that he went round her in a large circle.

Ellie found it strange not being in control. It reminded her of her very first riding lessons when George, the old groom, used to lead her on Shadow. But even then, she had held on to the reins. Now she wasn't quite sure what to do with her hands.

"Put your arms out to your sides," called Meg. "I want you to concentrate on balance today." She urged Sundance into a trot.

Princess Ellie and the Palace Plot

Ellie made herself rise up and down in
the saddle, in time with the pony's feet. She
was surprised how much more difficult it
was than when her hands were in front of
her. But Meg was right. Not having to worry
about controlling Sundance made it easier
to think about what her legs and body
were doing.

The Pony-Mad Princess

Round and round they went, first in one direction and then in the other. Each time they turned towards the palace, Ellie looked eagerly for a glimpse of Kate. Surely she would come soon. She wasn't usually this late.

Finally, as she was practising cantering without stirrups, Ellie spotted her friend running towards the sand school. She waved at her merrily, but Kate didn't wave back. She looked upset.

Meg stopped Sundance and Ellie jumped off. "Whatever's the matter?' she asked.

"I've been trying to calm my gran down," explained Kate. "But I can't. She's really cross. One of the maids fell over because of her silly

40

dress and she dropped a really special chocolate gateau that Gran had taken ages to make."

"It's Lord Leo's fault," grumbled Ellie. "He's upsetting everyone."

"Except your parents," said Kate.

Ellie sighed. "They think he's wonderful. He's convinced them that everyone will like the changes in the end."

"Gran won't and neither will Grandad," declared Kate. "They liked things the way they were. If everything's going to be different, they're not sure they want to stay at the palace."

Ellie stared at her in dismay. "But they can't leave. If they go, you'll go too."

"I know," cried Kate. "And I don't want to."

The Pony-Mad Princess

Ellie blinked back her tears. She had been so lonely before Kate came to live at the palace. If she went away, there'd be no one to play with and no one to share her ponies with. "We can't let it happen," she insisted. "We've got to do something to stop Lord Leo."

Chapter 5

Sundance nudged Ellie's arm with his nose and then did the same to Kate. "He's telling you both to cheer up," laughed Meg. "Now stop worrying and try to enjoy the rest of your lesson."

"It's Kate's turn to ride," said Ellie. She didn't mind watching for a while. She'd worked so hard that she was glad to have a break.

But she wasn't able to rest for long. As soon as Kate had practised walking and trotting in a circle, Meg called Ellie into the middle. "It's time you learned to lunge," she said. "It's a useful skill."

Ellie hesitated. Part of her was eager to try holding the lungeing-rein, but the rest of her was nervous. "Suppose something goes wrong?" she asked.

"It won't," said Meg. "Sundance is so sensible that the worst he'd do is stop. He's the perfect pony to learn with."

"And I'm still on him," added Kate. "If all else fails, I can pick up the reins and ride him normally."

Meg showed Ellie how to hold the lungeing-rein in one hand and the whip in the other. "Now use your voice to control him, just like you do when you're driving Shadow in his carriage."

"Walk on!" called Ellie, trying not to let her nervousness show. Sundance stepped forward obediently, walking in a large circle with her at the centre. She had to turn to keep facing him as he walked round. If she hadn't, she would have ended up with the lungeing-rein wound round her.

Sundance behaved so well that Ellie's confidence grew quickly. Soon, she had the pony trotting and cantering in circles while Kate practised riding without reins. Ellie was concentrating so hard that she didn't notice she had an audience until she heard her mother call, "Aurelia!"

She stopped Sundance and led him over to the fence where the King and Queen were standing with the new designer. He was wearing what Ellie decided must be his "walking in the country" outfit – green jacket, green shirt, green designer jeans and green wellington boots.

"We're just showing Lord Leo the palace grounds," explained the King.

"I hope you're not planning to change those too," said Ellie. She didn't want him

46

upsetting Meg as well as everyone else.

"Of course I'm not," he laughed. "I've much too much to do inside."

"Lord Leo's been telling us all about his wonderful home in the country," said the Queen. "You two girls should be interested. He has horses."

Ellie looked at him in surprise. This was the man who had frightened Angel. How could he know so little about horses if he had some of his own? "Tell us all about them," she asked, determined to solve the mystery.

"Oh, no!" replied Lord Leo. "I wouldn't dream of boring you."

"You won't," said Ellie. "I can listen to people talk about horses for hours."

"So can I," said Kate from her vantage

point on Sundance's back. "What are their names?"

Lord Leo hesitated as if he was having trouble remembering. "Now let me think. Umm…errr…there's Dobbin and Rover and Misty and Black Beauty."

Ellie's surprise grew. She had never heard such an unimaginative set of names. Her rocking horse had been called Dobbin, and Rover sounded like a better name for a dog. But she decided not to say anything. She wanted to find out more. "What colour are they?" she asked.

This time Lord Leo seemed more confident. "Black Beauty's black, of course. Misty is white. And Rover is exactly the same shade of brown as this pretty little pony."

Before he had time to describe Dobbin,

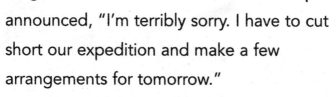

his mobile phone started playing the national anthem. He pulled it out and listened to the message. Then he smiled apologetically at the King and Queen and announced, "I'm terribly sorry. I have to cut short our expedition and make a few arrangements for tomorrow."

Ellie watched him walk back to the palace with her parents. Then she turned to Kate and asked, "How can anyone with horses have trouble remembering their names?"

"Or think Sundance is brown, not chestnut?" replied Kate.

"Or say their horse is white, instead of grey," added Ellie.

Kate looked thoughtful. "Maybe he doesn't really know anything about horses. That would explain why he hooted at Angel yesterday and frightened her."

"But that would mean he's making it all up," said Ellie. "And if he's lying about the horses, maybe he's lying about other things as well…"

Chapter 6

The more Ellie and Kate thought about Lord Leo, the more suspicious they became.

"Maybe he's pretending to know about design," suggested Kate. "That would explain why the new staff uniforms are so awful."

Ellie nodded thoughtfully. "Perhaps he's not related to Leonardo da Vinci either."

"But why would he lie about that?" asked Kate.

Ellie shrugged. "Maybe he likes to sound important. It certainly works. That's why Mum and Dad trust him so much."

Kate grinned. "Then you've got to tell them. If they find out he's lying, they might send him away and everything will go back to normal."

Ellie was sure her friend was right. But she didn't have a chance to speak to her parents on their own until the evening. She waited until Lord Leo was busy looking at the oil paintings in the corridor. Then she crept into the parlour without letting him see her.

The King and Queen were sitting in their comfy thrones, sipping tea from china cups while they played chess. They looked up in surprise when Ellie came in. "Do you want a game?" asked the Queen.

Ellie shook her head. "I need to talk to you about Lord Leo."

"Not again," complained the King. "You've already made it quite clear that you don't like what he's doing."

"But we do understand how you feel,

53

Aurelia," added the Queen, with a sympathetic smile. "Lord Leo has explained that little children always resist change at first."

Ellie felt a wave of anger. "I'm not a little child," she cried. Then she forced herself to calm down and added in a quieter voice, "He's lying about having horses."

The King slowly lowered his cup onto his saucer and stared at her. "That's a very serious thing to say, Aurelia. I hope you can prove it."

"Of course I can," declared Ellie. "He said one of his horses was white, instead of grey, and he said Sundance was brown instead of chestnut."

"That sounds perfectly reasonable to me," laughed the Queen. "He likes to be up to date. So it's natural for him to use modern names for colours rather than traditional horsey ones."

The King gave Ellie a reassuring hug. "There's nothing to worry about. Your mother and I know what we're doing and so does Lord Leo. The whole palace is going to be so wonderfully modern and completely up to date."

Ellie knew she wasn't going to persuade them. But she was sure she was right. The designer wasn't telling the truth and she was determined to find out why.

The next morning was Saturday, so Ellie didn't have any lessons. But no one else seemed to be taking the day off. The palace was a hive of activity. All the maids were

hobbling about in their new dresses, trying
to cover the carpets with dustsheets.

Ellie spotted Higginbottom in the
entrance hall. He was still wearing his lion
tamer outfit, so she crept up behind him,
planning to roar fiercely and make him jump.

But at the last minute, she changed her
mind. He was already so upset that it didn't

seem fair to make fun of him. Instead, she just asked, "What's going on?"

The butler smiled and gave a small bow. "It's Lord Leo again, Your Highness. His men will be here in a minute to start the decorating."

Ellie looked round. Apart from the dustsheets, the palace looked exactly the same as usual. "But you're not ready yet. You've still got all the paintings to take down, the ornaments to put away and the furniture to move."

Higginbottom sighed. "Apparently *they're* going to move everything. We weren't supposed to do anything at all. But I insisted on the dustsheets. I don't want their dirty feet trampling all over our clean carpets."

As he finished speaking, an enormous

lorry drew up at the palace entrance. A gang of men in brown overalls jumped out and swung open the large doors at the back. With perfect timing, Lord Leo drove up beside them. His red sports car sent up a spray of gravel as it screeched to a halt.

He jumped out and started issuing orders. Then he noticed Ellie watching him from the doorway and his voice dropped to a whisper. The men huddled round him so they could hear.

As soon as Lord Leo had finished talking, they set to work unloading a variety of boxes, stepladders and tins of paint. Soon, there were men everywhere carrying things in and out of the palace. They were extremely interested in all the ornaments and pictures. They peered at the signatures on the paintings and lifted up the silver statues to read the hallmarks on their bases. One of them even produced a magnifying glass so he could see them better.

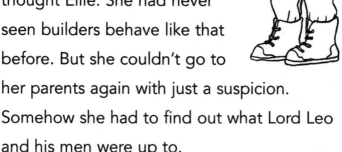

"I don't trust them," thought Ellie. She had never seen builders behave like that before. But she couldn't go to her parents again with just a suspicion. Somehow she had to find out what Lord Leo and his men were up to.

Chapter 7

"Are you sure this is going to work?" asked Kate, as she led Angel towards the enormous lorry.

"It's got to," said Ellie. "We need to keep an eye on what they're doing and Angel is the perfect excuse."

Angel arched her neck and blew down her nose as she stared curiously at the lorry. Kate stroked the foal's face to reassure her. "It's all right," she whispered. "It's not going to hurt you."

"It's only a lorry," added Ellie. She patted Angel's neck and felt the foal relax. Then she turned to Kate and said, "Don't stop. We need to get closer so we can see better."

They led Angel round the back of the huge vehicle. Lord Leo was still there, supervising his men as they moved things in and out of the palace. As the girls arrived, one of the workmen stomped inside the lorry carrying two tins of paint. His footsteps made so much noise on the wooden ramp that Angel stepped back in surprise.

"Steady, girl," soothed Ellie.

Lord Leo spun round to see who was talking. A brief look of annoyance showed on his face before he replaced it with a wide smile. "Good morning, Princess Aurelia. I'm surprised you're not out riding on such a wonderful day."

Ellie smiled back, trying hard to give the impression of complete innocence. "We're giving Angel a lesson," she explained. "Your lorry is the ideal way to teach her to be confident in traffic."

"It's very useful practice," added Kate. "You've already seen how nervous she is."

"Of course, I have," replied Lord Leo. He waved a hand at them dismissively. "But do try to stay out of everyone's way."

They turned Angel away from the lorry and led her round in a large circle. As they walked, Ellie whispered, "Did you see what that man was carrying?"

"Tins of paint," said Kate. "But there's nothing strange about that. He's a decorator."

"But why would he be carrying them *into* the lorry?" asked Ellie. "They've only just been carried out of it."

Kate scratched her head thoughtfully with the end of Angel's lead rope. "Perhaps they were the wrong colour."

That was such a boring explanation that Ellie didn't want to admit it might be true. She preferred to think they might have stumbled

63

on an amazing plot like the children always did in her pony books. "There's only one way to find out the truth," replied Ellie. "We'll have to put the rest of the plan into action."

They walked Angel round in another large circle while they waited for the right moment. It came when Lord Leo went back inside the palace, taking three of the men with him. With fewer people around, there would be less chance of getting caught.

"Now," whispered Ellie. She slipped away from Kate and Angel and pressed herself flat against the far side of the lorry where she couldn't be seen from the palace. She crossed her fingers tightly, hoping no one would walk round and see her hiding there.

Princess Ellie and the Palace Plot

A few seconds later, Kate gave a loud, remarkably convincing cry of pain. Ellie peeped round the corner of the lorry and saw everyone was staring at her friend. She was hopping on one foot, holding the other one, in a wonderful imitation of someone who had just been trodden on by a foal.

Ellie knew this was her chance. No one was looking at the lorry. So she summoned all her courage, tiptoed up the ramp and crept inside. It was darker than she'd expected and the stuffy air was tinged with the sharp scents of new wood and paint.

The floor was covered with a muddle of boxes and packages. Close to one wall stood the two paint tins they had seen carried in. At least, she hoped these were the tins. It was hard to tell, but they were on their own, away from the other decorating supplies. There must be something special about them.

She picked up one of the tins and shook it gently. A thrill of excitement ran down her spine as she heard something rattle inside – something that definitely wasn't paint. With her heart racing, she picked up a screwdriver from the floor and started to lever off the lid.

Suddenly she heard a footstep on the ramp and froze with fear. Someone was coming into the lorry. Now she was in real trouble.

Chapter 8

Ellie struggled to stay calm. She and Kate had known she might get caught. That's why they'd planned what she should do next. But whether it would work depended on how good she was at acting.

She put down the screwdriver and stood up quietly as the footsteps came closer. She had to fight back her natural instinct to run

away or hide. Either of those actions would
instantly make her look guilty.

Instead, she peered behind a large box
and called, "Here, kitty, kitty, kitty!"

"What are you up to?" shouted a deep
voice.

She swung round and saw
a large workman blocking
her way out of the lorry.
Her stomach was
knotted with fear but she
knew she mustn't show it.
She smiled as innocently as
she could and announced,
"I'm looking for the cat."

"What cat?" asked
the man.

"The one that frightened

Angel and made her jump on Kate's foot," Ellie explained. "I saw it run in here and I thought I should get it out before you drive away."

To her surprise, the man smiled. "That's very sweet of you, my love. But you'd better leave that to me. Now, hoppit. We can't have princesses climbing round in here getting hurt. My governor would never hear the last of it from the health and safety people."

Ellie did as she was told, delighted that she could escape so easily. As soon as she was outside she ran to join Kate who was limping convincingly towards the stables with Angel. From inside the lorry, they could hear the workman calling, "Here, little kitty. Come to daddykins."

Princess Ellie and the Palace Plot

Kate giggled. "I can't believe that worked. I was so scared when I saw him going up the ramp."

"So was I," said Ellie. "We got away with it though. But we still haven't found out what's going on. There was definitely something in one of those tins, but I didn't have time to see what it was."

Kate groaned. "I don't care how important this is. I'm not doing that again."

Ellie knew she was right. They couldn't try the same trick twice. But there must be some way to show her parents that Lord Leo was up to no good.

By lunchtime, the clearing of the palace was well under way. All the paintings and ornaments in the entrance hall had already disappeared. Ellie wondered how many of them were in the storage barns and how many were hidden in the lorry.

Lord Leo was full of confidence during the meal. Dressed in green as usual, he boasted about his wonderful home, his yacht and his private plane. As he spoke, he waved his hands around dramatically to emphasize his words, making life extremely difficult for the maids who were serving the food.

"And the house is surrounded by beautiful countryside," he declared, swinging both arms wide. His left hand narrowly missed the coffee pot

Higginbottom was carrying, but Lord Leo didn't seem to notice.

"It must be perfect for riding," said the Queen.

"Oh, yes," he gushed. "I ride every day when I'm at home."

"Liar," thought Ellie. Then she had an idea. If *she* couldn't prove Lord Leo was making things up, perhaps she could help him prove it himself. "Perhaps you'd like a ride on one of my ponies," she suggested.

But he wasn't going to be trapped that easily. "What a kind offer," he beamed. "It's such a pity your ponies are too small for me."

"But they're not," replied Ellie. "Starlight's much bigger than the others. She could carry you easily."

"Oh," said Lord Leo. His smile vanished for a moment and he seemed lost for words. Then he beamed again and said, "I'd love to ride her, but unfortunately I've left all my riding clothes at home."

To Ellie's delight, the King patted Lord Leo on the shoulder and declared, "Nonsense, my dear chap. After all you've done for us, I wouldn't dream of letting you miss your ride over such a tiny problem."

He called out to Higginbottom. "Take the royal car to town and buy Lord Leo the best riding outfit you can find. And be as quick as you can."

"Certainly, Your Majesty," replied the butler. He gave a deep bow and left. On the way out, he glanced at Ellie and she was surprised to see a hint of mischief in his eyes.

Princess Ellie and the Palace Plot

"You must have your ride this afternoon," said the Queen. "You're working so hard that you deserve a break."

"Thank you," said Lord Leo in a very quiet voice. He seemed to have lost his usual confidence and the slightly green tinge to his face wasn't just the reflection from his clothes.

Ellie slipped quietly away from the table. She had things to organize. If her plan was going to work, this would have to be a very special ride.

Chapter 9

Ellie and Kate groomed Starlight until her coat shone. Then they brushed all the tangles out of her mane and tail and made sure there wasn't a speck of mud on the long, shaggy hairs that hung over her hooves.

Kate pointed at them and smiled. "I bet Lord Leo doesn't know they're called feathers."

"I can't complain about that," laughed Ellie. "I didn't know either until Meg told me."

She heard the crunch of tyres on the drive as a car drove past. "That sounds like Higginbottom coming back. I'll go and check."

She ran over to the palace and caught up with the butler just as he met Lord Leo in the entrance hall.

Higginbottom bowed respectfully and handed over a large box. It was made of gold card with "Fantastic Fashions for the Fabulous" printed across it in blue, twirly writing.

Lord Leo put on a reasonably convincing show of gratitude. But, as he pulled each item out of the box, he looked more and more dismayed. None of the clothes were green.

The jacket and jodhpurs were bright orange and so was the silk cover for the riding hat.

He glared at Higginbottom. "How could you?" he snapped. "You must know my taste in colour. It's so obvious."

The butler's face lit up with a smile of satisfaction. "But green is so last year," he purred.

Ellie clamped her hand over her mouth to stop herself laughing. Lord Leo looked stunned. Before he had time to say anything, the King and Queen swept into the hall and he changed his expression to a forced grin.

The King beamed back. "Good. I see your outfit's arrived." He turned and smiled at Ellie. "Should Lord Leo meet you at the stables, Aurelia?"

"The sand school would be better," replied Ellie. "Why don't you both come and watch."

"What an excellent idea," said the Queen.

"Please don't feel you have to," suggested Lord Leo, with a hint of desperation in his voice. "I wouldn't be at all offended if you didn't."

"I know you wouldn't," said the King. "But it will give us great pleasure to see you enjoying yourself."

When she got back to the stables, Ellie

found Kate had already put on Starlight's saddle and bridle. So she fetched the cavesson from the tack room, adjusted it to fit the bay mare's head and buckled it into place.

Meg buckled on the lungeing-rein and handed it to Ellie. "Just remember everything I've taught you. Starlight's as good as gold when she's lunged. You shouldn't have any problems."

They arrived at the sand school at the same time as the royal party. The King and Queen were in the lead, followed by two footmen carrying folding thrones, a rainbow of maids carrying refreshments, and Higginbottom. The butler wasn't carrying anything and Ellie suspected he was just here to watch the fun.

Lord Leo was walking slightly behind the King and Queen. The forced grin was still on his face, but his shoulders drooped miserably inside his orange jacket.

Kate nudged Ellie with her elbow. "He looks like a giant carrot," she whispered.

Ellie giggled. "I hope Starlight doesn't notice." Carrots were the pony's favourite treat.

She stepped forward and welcomed Lord Leo into the sand school. "I thought we'd start you off on the lunge," she explained, holding up the lungeing-rein to explain what she was talking about. "That'll give you a chance to get used to Starlight."

She thought she detected a glimmer of relief in his eyes as he realized he'd be led. That swiftly vanished when she continued, "Then we can go for a good gallop across the deer park and do some jumping on our cross-country course."

Lord Leo gulped, but managed to keep the forced grin on his face. "I suppose I'd better get on," he said, walking round to Starlight's right-hand side.

Kate gave a polite cough. "It's usual to *mount* from the left," she remarked.

"I know that," he replied quickly. He gave Starlight's neck a nervous pat and moved to the other side, muttering, "I was just checking all the stirrupy bits were there."

Meg hurried over carrying a large box. "Perhaps you'd like to use a mounting block," she suggested. Then she turned to Ellie and whispered, "He doesn't seem to know what he's doing. I don't think you'll get him on without it."

Lord Leo climbed onto the box and put his right foot in the stirrup. For a wonderful moment, Ellie thought he was going to end

up sitting on Starlight, facing her tail. But he wasn't quite that stupid. After a moment's thought, he took his right foot out again, put his left foot in instead and swung himself into the saddle the right way round.

That was the only thing he did right. His toes pointed down, his heels pointed up.

His back slumped like a sack of potatoes and he held the reins so high that he looked like a dog begging for a biscuit.

Princess Ellie and the Palace Plot

Ellie realized with delight that her suspicions were correct. Lord Leo had no idea how to ride. He was hopeless sitting still and, if her plan worked properly, he would be in an even worse mess when Starlight started to move. The King and Queen would be sure to notice that he didn't know what he was doing. Then they would have to believe that he hadn't told them the truth.

Chapter 10

Ellie gently prised the reins from Lord Leo's fingers and tied them in a knot. "You won't need those for a while," she explained.

He immediately transferred his grip to the front of the saddle. "Fine," he squeaked, in a strangely high-pitched voice. His grin was now so fixed that his teeth stayed clamped together even when he spoke.

Princess Ellie and the Palace Plot

Ellie took the lungeing-rein in one hand and the whip in the other. Then she stepped away from Starlight and made the bay mare walk round in a large circle. It seemed fair to give Lord Leo a chance to get his balance.

After a few steps, he seemed to realize that sitting on a walking horse wasn't that difficult. He relaxed and looked more confident. His grin looked more natural, and he let go of the saddle.

A small crowd had gathered beside the sand school. The men from the lorry had abandoned their work and drifted over to see what was happening. Miss Stringle had come, too, and so had several of the palace guards. The King and Queen smiled and waved as Lord Leo rode past.

Ellie waited until Lord Leo was in the middle of waving back. Then she urged Starlight into a bouncy trot.

"Oooh!" he squealed, as he grabbed hold of the saddle again.

"It's good you can already ride," called Ellie. "Trotting is so uncomfortable if you can't."

"I know," cried Lord Leo. His bottom bumped painfully around in the saddle because he didn't know how to rise up and down in time with Starlight's feet.

Starlight trotted round and round, faster and faster. The quicker she went, the harder Lord Leo bumped. Soon his back slumped with exhaustion and his grin finally disappeared. "Can we stop now?" he cried.

"Not yet!" called Ellie. "We've only just begun." She urged Starlight into a canter.

The sudden change of pace knocked the designer off balance. His left foot slipped out of its stirrup and he slid sideways in the saddle. "Oh, no!" he wailed.

The King leaped to his feet. "Lord Leo's in trouble. Slow the pony down, Aurelia."

Ellie did as she was told. Starlight obediently stopped cantering and started to trot again.

But that didn't help Lord Leo. He bumped harder than ever. He gripped the saddle so hard that his knuckles turned white. "Please stop!" he begged.

"In a minute," Ellie promised. "But first I think you have something to tell my parents."

Lord Leo slipped further out of the saddle.

He threw his arms round Starlight's neck to save himself and stared desperately at Ellie. "I don't know what you mean," he cried.

"Just tell everyone the truth," said Ellie.

Lord Leo was clinging onto Starlight like a monkey and looked as if he was about to burst into tears. "Okay, okay," he wailed. "I'm not a lord, I'm not a designer and I'm nothing to do with Leonardo da Vinci."

Most of the crowd gasped in horror.

Princess Ellie and the Palace Plot

The only ones that didn't were the gang of workmen. They started to creep quietly back to the lorry, but they soon found their way blocked by the palace guards.

The King ignored them. He was busy concentrating on Lord Leo. "Who are you then?" he demanded.

Ellie stopped Starlight, and watched the fake designer slide off into the sand. Then she pointed at him and declared, "He's a thief. I'm sure he is. Just look in his lorry and see."

"We certainly will," agreed the Queen, her eyes wide with shock. "Guards, fetch that man and follow us." She walked briskly back towards the palace with the King. Two of the guards lifted Lord Leo to his feet and marched him after them. Ellie and Kate followed close behind with Starlight.

As soon as they reached the lorry, Ellie jumped inside and found the tin she'd failed to open earlier. She held it up and shook it. "Listen," she said. "Paint doesn't rattle like that."

The sergeant of the palace guard drew his ornamental sword and used it to prise the lid off the tin. Ellie watched him anxiously. Suppose she was wrong? Suppose Lord Leo wasn't a thief and all that was inside was a screwdriver? Then she would look really foolish.

As soon as the lid was off, she reached inside the tin. To her relief, she didn't find a screwdriver. Instead, her fingers closed round an object that felt very familiar. She pulled it out and saw that she was right. It was her favourite statue of the flying horse, looking more beautiful than ever as it glittered in the sunlight.

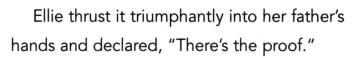

Ellie thrust it triumphantly into her father's hands and declared, "There's the proof."

The King waved the statue angrily at Lord Leo. "You're under arrest. Your plot has failed."

"I know," muttered Lord Leo. He looked utterly miserable as the palace guards led him away.

The King smiled sheepishly at Ellie. "I'm sorry we didn't believe you before."

"Will we have to have another designer?" asked Ellie. "I think I've had enough change to last me for ages."

"So have I," laughed the Queen.

The King laughed too. "Perhaps makeovers aren't as important as I thought." He turned to the servants and announced, "I think we'll go back to the old uniforms. In future, we'll stick to tradition."

"Brilliant," said Kate. "Now Gran won't be cross any more."

"And you won't have to move," said Ellie. She felt very happy. Everything was back the way it ought to be – or it would be as soon as Higginbottom stopped looking like a lion tamer.

The King put his arm round her shoulders. "We're very proud of you," he said.

"You've saved the palace treasure," added the Queen.

Ellie pulled a carrot out of her pocket and gave it to the bay mare. "But I couldn't have done it without Kate and Starlight," she said.

The Pony-Mad Princess

Princess Ellie to the Rescue
ISBN: 0 7460 6018 1
Can Ellie save her beloved pony, Sundance, when he goes missing?

Princess Ellie's Secret
ISBN: 0 7460 6019 X
Ellie comes up with a secret plan to stop Shadow from being sold.

A Puzzle for Princess Ellie
ISBN: 0 7460 6020 3
Why won't Rainbow go down the spooky woodland path?

Princess Ellie's Starlight Adventure
ISBN: 0 7460 6021 1
Hoofprints appear on the palace lawn and Ellie has to find the culprit.

Princess Ellie's Moonlight Mystery
ISBN: 0 7460 6022 X
Ellie is enjoying pony camp, until she hears noises in the night.

A Surprise for Princess Ellie
ISBN: 0 7460 6023 8
Ellie sets off in search of adventure, but ends up with a big surprise.

Princess Ellie's Holiday Adventure
ISBN: 0 7460 6732 1
Ellie and Kate go to visit Prince John, and get lost in the snow!

Princess Ellie and the Palace Plot
ISBN: 0 7460 6733 X
Can Ellie's pony, Starlight, help her uncover the palace plot?

Princess Ellie's Christmas
ISBN: 0 7460 6833 6
Ellie's plan for the perfect Christmas present goes horribly wrong...

Princess Ellie Saves the Day
ISBN: 0 7460 6834 4
Can Ellie save the day when one of her ponies gets ill?

Princess Ellie's Summer Holiday
ISBN: 0 7460 7308 9
Wilfred the Wonder Dog is missing and it's up to Ellie to find him.